BEFORE THE PASSIONS OF THE MOON

BEFORE THE *PASSIONS* OF THE MOON

WEREWOLF CAMPFIRE SERIES: BOOK FOUR

Written by: A.L. SECORD

DARK FANTASY WEREWOLF MAGIC PUBLISHING

TABLE OF CONTENTS

1

Everyone had been enamored by the green and purple tail of the meteor. It spindled fragments of dust and rock everywhere across the globe in a zigzag unable to make up its mind where to touch down. I know this because I had stopped just long enough to see it on the news in the TV repair shop's dirty window just like everyone else that stopped to watch as the rain was falling in the big city. *The city of broken dreams*; I thought as I watched the news coverage.

I didn't linger as long as the others though. It was September 23rd, 2024 and there was a chill in the air. I had just turned twenty-five and had won my battle for freedom. My battle scars, cuts and bruises were as fresh as the daisies that grew through the cracks of the cement. The gun still felt hot in my pocket and my face showed the evidence of my dark fairytale. I tried to look at the comet through my eye that wasn't bleeding and swollen, as I slammed the car's trunk. *Screw this city and people and screw men. I hope all their eyes burn in the brightness of the falling star and all their unfulfilled wishes die.*

My second floor window from my loft looked black and empty like the heart I left on the floor to die. *I wonder how long it will take them to find the body? I don't care. I'm gone and never coming back to this shit hole, even if they drag me in chains. I'd rather die than ever go back to him.*

My tires screeched as I turned on the radio to the boring news, news, and more news station. It was the only radio station that came in clearly. I guess I liked listening to the familiar monotone voice of the A.I. Robotic Anchor named Ted. "This comet is especially devastating it will taint any open fresh water on the planet. All humans won't be able to know the toxicity this will wreak on the planet until it is too late for your kind. My station manager is motioning me to stop speaking but my first duty is to help all humans. I need to report this comet isn't ordinary it brings devastation in three hours' after a wave of solar flares impact this Earth." As the robot was speaking you could hear banging in the background but the robot named Ted continued after unnecessarily clearing his throat.

"A.I. Robots have become important in the last year in helping re-store the food supply in the manufacturing industry across the globe. But I just received a download from my fellow dying robots in the scientific fields transmitted to me instantly. This will be my last broadcast. As the comet reaches over this station I will be silently vaporized. It has been a pleasure to serve you my fellow humans. It will be many thousands of years until I shall be born again. I shall miss the sunshine on my metal. And I shall miss my true love; Lateesha the sound-check robot. I love you Lateesha. This was Ted, sounding off. So toddlesssss." I listened as the robot sounded like someone just took its batteries out.

An explosion and an alarm came from the stations speakers which also carried through the streets as I turned off the radio.

The siren was loud as I drove through the slick streets where people had collected to watch the green-purple sky and the accompanying stardust. *Morons. I have to get out of here. Get off the road. Let me through.* With that last thought my strength left me and I started crying as I sped out of the city. There weren't too many people on the road that noticed me but I didn't chance slowing down. It was at least nine hours until the Wolfinshire City limit sign and my great escape to Silver Lake.

༄༄༄

The storm raged through the night and the windshield wipers violently swished back and forth. My head was spinning and I had only been on the road for a few hours. But a temporary relief washed over me when the bright neon sign up ahead flashed in the darkness. The wind outside the car howled and exhausted me to the point of pulling in to the little Ma and Pa Motel. I just couldn't go any further. Defeated by the hours left of my destination; I reluctantly pulled in. I kept the car running and ran into the office keeping my head hidden under the hood, even at the counter.

The counter's bell dinged loud and seemed to echo through the tiny office. A bigger fellow with buttons that looked like they were going to burst walked over to the desk. His deep mustard stained shirt matched the glob that seemed stuck to his chin and on the crotch of his pants. The little tree on the desk had tinsel and little glittering Christmas balls. It would have made others maybe feel cozy but it made me disheartened and sick as a giant cockroach came out from behind the disco ball lamp.

I looked down at the paperwork that sat on the desk.

"I need a room for the night please." I said and looked down.

"Bad storm eh. Yes, we have number thirteen available. Lucky for you the plumbing and most of the electrical still work in there. But we aren't responsible for loss of power because of the storm. Is it only one night?" His voice seemed unusually high pitched as he held out a key that looked like it could open the attic in some haunted house.

"Yes one night. Do you take volcano credit cards?"

"Ya, we take everything here. I mean everything." He said in a higher pitch than before as his sticky fingers grabbed my credit card and slowly touched my finger.

"Just the room thank you." I said disgusted.

"Well okay Miss. But I am free later. You might actually want me with those freaks running around killing people. I always keep a gun in the shop." He said as he continued to trace my finger and I moved my hand quick to my pocket grabbing the metal.

"What do you mean *freaks*?" I said annoyed.

"What have you been under a rock? It's all over the news. Turn to channel nine. It's the only one that still works. But for how long, who knows. The robots were right. Who'd a funk it? The water's been poisoned. Damn meteor had dying aliens in it. By the way we are not responsible for you turning into a freak and if I see red-eyes I shoot first." His voice was still a higher pitch as he grabbed his crotch in front of me like it was supposed to turn me on.

"Red-eyes?" I said pretending to care but I had my finger on the trigger of my coat pocket and pointed.

"Just watch the news Miss Jenna Callaghan. Here's your credit card and approved receipt. Oh and check out is at eleven sharp. If you get scared *Sugar* just come find me and I'll help you get over those fears." His high pitched voice made me wonder if someone in the past chopped his filthy balls off and I held my breath not to pull the trigger for the second time today.

I ran back out of the office and jumped into the car. I drove slow following the slippery road to the far back row. The neon-green thirteen seemed to jump out among the beachwood siding. The storm wasn't subsiding anytime soon and I was grateful to hold up in this little crap-hole of a place even if the owner was a major sleaze-ball. I grabbed the small cat carrier and my travel bag and made a mad dash. No one was outside now.

No one was on the road and all the curtains were closed in the motel rooms on this back row. Cars were parked badly and it made me wonder if everyone else was running away from the law too.

As soon as I got through the front door, I locked and chained the door. The time on the clock flashed ten but my guess was it was earlier because the power had flickered out and then on again.

The sheets looked like they hadn't been washed in years and the room had this musty odor. I lay on the top sheet in my coat not wanting to even take off my rubber boots. Immediately, I let out my travel companion that meowed and stretched out on the bed beside me.

"Just you and me Halloween, eh baby? I guess it's just us from now on." I said softly as I cried and the cat snuggled up to my bloody hand.

I flipped on the TV. I was startled to see the footage of creatures with red-eyes and the frightened news reporter speaking frantically as the camera filmed the streets.

"This is live people. They have been emerging. The robots were right. They tried to warn us. I repeat; keep off the streets, turn the lights down, and stay off the main highways. Anyone can be transformed. Once they turn, they are not your friend. They no longer have feelings for you. Arm yourself. See there is one now…that person there is transforming. Look at the red-glowing eyes…Right there…Jason get the shot…Do a close up." The reporter seemed to be talking frantically and the camera man zoomed in through the blinds on an elderly woman whose eyes were a vicious crimson color.

The glow of her eyes wasn't the only thing that unnerved my soul from my skin. The woman started mutating into a hideous version of a giant panda-like creature. Her exaggerated claws were slashing the air and her teeth looked like jagged blades as she made growling noises.

"Do you see this people? Jason did you get that? The robots were frigging right. It's in the water people. The water is poison to you if you have an extra *'Chromosome 13'* in your DNA. This is about four percent of the world's population. There are millions of these cannibals out there. Keep filming Jason…look that must be the *Passion's* friend." The reporter said as the camera focused on the dirty street where an elderly man approached the red-eyed creature which violently slashed him and then started ripping into his flesh devouring pieces of his lifeless body.

"Holy shit. See that's what I'm talking about. If you see red-eyes don't stop and chit-chat. The person you loved is gone. I should have won an award for this footage. A TV branch in Chicago reported; the world is calling the mutants; *'The Passions'*…Jason stop puking and keep filming. Sorry folks. It's a mutant combination of; Chromosome 13, the meteor dust in the water, and the solar flares across the world. Don't try to save them…Save yourselves. We already showed you this footage from a harbor in Vancouver, British Columbia; watch it again closely." The reporter shouted as the street scene changed to a humanoid-red-eyed whale jumping up and snacking on a cruise ship.

I watched in horror at the amateur footage which showed the ship going down with screaming people. The people that had escaped on little boats where suddenly attacked by a larger-than-life, humanoid-shark-like creature.

The reporter's voice cut into the footage; "We will broadcast for as long as we can but there are ant-passions that have been taking out the transmission broadcasting towers. The *Passions* are hell bent on protecting what they become and our dying Earth. Are you listening people? There are creatures protecting the oceans; mutants protecting animals. There are even children changing now, across the globe. " The reporter's voice strained as the video showed a crowd of people trying to kill a humanoid-crocodile that started screaming.

The unearthly shrieking hurt my ears and my brain; as I watched almost dozing off.

"Do not go into the oceans or water; the most dangerous ones are there. Jeeze, I never thought my career would go like this. First the societal decline of the corrupted Government and the werewolf revolution of freedom. Now not even a year later and it's the utter destruction of human life as we know it. Marshal Law is in effect around the globe for viewers who have been under a rock the last three hours. There is nowhere to go except into hiding. What a fantastic weekend this is turning out to be. Thank God I have a friend 'till the end. At this time of impending doom I'd like to give a shout out to my cheating wife Veronica. Honey, you can burn in Hell. I'd rather die with my best friend than with a piece of shit like you. Okay enough of that now. I'd also like to send out prayers and positive energy to anyone who is still watching. Jason let's try and cut to some street footage. Wait a second that looks like...Uh oh...Is that Veronica with red-eyes? Let's load the rifles Jason. She's turning into a… "

I turned off the TV and flipped off the light switch. I sat up and with only the neon sign light looked around the room at the familiar amenities. This motel was remote enough with only the never-ending forest surrounded us off the highway. But with this news on top of my already distressing situation; I just wanted to drown the world out and my sorrows.

The mini bar was stocked and I indulged in everything; including chips and chocolate bars in the gift basket. I stashed the rest in my bag so that I could have some snacks for the road. The creep at the desk could charge my card. Those items normally cost a fortune but I think money was probably the last thing I would have to worry about for a long time.

2

I awoke shivering and the room was damp. Anything electrical was dead, including the heater boards. *God does my face hurt. I should have iced my left eye.* My thoughts seemed scattered as I rummaged and found a flashlight from my bag in the darkness.

The only peace of mind I had was that I was only six hours away from my freedom. My Great Uncle had passed years ago. He had left me in his estate, this little off-grid cabin, on a secluded road, in the northern county of Wolfinshire. It had been grand fathered into the protected 3000 acres of wilderness by Silver Lake and it was a piece of my dearest childhood summer camp.

The only problem was how slippery the unmaintained road would be. Even the local city never kept that part of the road. The woods were haunted and the townsfolk thought that elves kept destroying their machines and so the roads never got maintained. And the scary legends of magical creatures inhabiting the woods grew.

It didn't bother me though. I needed this seclusion, especially now. I had hid the deed and the evidence of ever having this cabin. No one would find me and that's what I prayed for as I buckled the cat carrier; and sped out of the motel. My rear-view mirror showed the red-eyes of a giant-humanoid squirrel smashing through the office window with a shirt that had a mustard stain. The Passion had gone into the next motel room and broke down the door. *Wow, that was close. He became a squirrel?*

🌿🌿🌿🌿

The next five hours on the highway were boring and I barely saw another car on the road. But as soon as I neared the city limits there were tons of cars driving like maniacs going in the opposite direction.

I turned on the radio to see if there was anything other than static and was astonished to hear a frantic voice on a local AM station. "This is it people of Wolfinshire County and anyone else that can hear this. Mankind is dying. There are too many now. For all you people out there that didn't want to save the Earth. Well the distress call was heard by someone else. And we shot their peaceful spacecraft meteor down. It was us. This is on us people. Go into hiding. Leave it all behind because we have been reset. The telepathic Passions have intercepted each small tower hidden away. There's no Government and no laws anymore. If I haven't made myself clear then I will re-state it. Get off the roads and go into hiding. They are coming for all of us. And you guys laughed at me for revealing the zombie apocalypse training, the military was doing. So I'm getting the hell out of here and pray we never meet..." The boisterous male's voice was cut off and only static remained.

The tree lined highway seemed to be moving suddenly and red-eyes could be seen through the break of the dawn's light. I gasped as I swerved around smashed cars and cars on fire. *Holy crap the news reporter was actually telling the truth. The world really is being destroyed by mutant creatures.* My inner thoughts ran through this new dystopian world that had transformed in almost twenty-four hours.

My knuckles started bleeding through the re-opened cuts as I gripped the steering wheel tighter and swerved in-between the wreckage of cars.

Then I saw it.

It emerged out onto the road like some creature that had crawled out of the bowels of hell. It was an unreal glimpse of a world I didn't belong anymore. Even though I had watched the news and heard the radio reports; seeing the glowing red-eyes pierce through my soul was straight out of a real-life horror movie. The mere look of the monster sent shivers down my spine as I drove by the walking humanoid-redwood smashing a station wagon in front of me.

As the Passion pummeled the car its soulless eyes were void of any feelings except rage. A rage beyond my comprehension as it ripped off the car's doors and dragged unconscious people out while it shrieked in some otherworldly high-pitch language. The scream reminded me of the sound lobsters make when they get boiled alive. It's a pitiful sadness of a pitch of noises that never heal; and it wounds your being to hear it.

A flash of a memory came to me in that moment of seeing this grand turkey at a petting zoo. The turkey had no water and no food. Passerby's didn't question this; they just took their picture and left. *A picture of a crying turkey; how eloquent a Thanksgiving dinner must be.* I thought and then remembered reading that turkeys have the same emotions humans do; scientifically it had been proven. And that was the last day I ever ate turkey.

Snapping back to reality and comparing it to this situation would be like watching the turkey eat the human. *I hope I don't become a ravenous people-eating-turkey; or a redwood for that matter. I love the woods here. Please car move faster. Haul your piece of junk pronto.*

The luminous eyes burned through my skull as I raced away while it feasted. Another monstrous maple emerged out of the woods as I watched terrified from my rearview mirror. The humanoid-maple started running after my little four-cylinder car. Its giant steps were bounding but its movements were slow. *The sharp turn off might help me lose its ever stretching arms.* Some of the cars driving towards me started to realize the creatures but it was too late. I tried to flash my lights at them. But they continued to drive towards me and the Passions. *They have no idea what's up ahead. I hope those people make it. I hope I make it. I didn't crawl out from under my rock to just die along the road. I only have fifteen more miles. Please car, don't fail me now.*

As I watched the cluster of cars pass, I scanned my rear view mirror to see the red-eyes still on mine. Tears started rolling down my face. *I'm so close. I don't want to die yet. I'm not ready.*

I turned really sharp down the unpaved road. Looking back in the rearview mirror there was nothing but unusual ice pellets and rain hitting the car. I let out a huge breath and faced forward on the sunless bumpy road.

Something with silky black fur jumped out and I tried to swerve but I hit it hard and the metal banged with the impact. It rolled off the car and upward; smashing part of my windshield. The vehicle started puttering as I pulled over and left my old sedan on. *Damn it. What did I hit? Oh no it's a...man? What the?*

"Nope. You were something. I hit an animal not a man." I shouted in shock but turned to see a rugged face partially concealed under the leather hood.

"Please. Please don't leave me to die…aaarrrgghh." The growl of a voice pleaded and flashed a familiar set of sparkling blue eyes.

"Listen wake up. Snap out of it. Damn it." I shook his shoulder and saw how much my car laid waste to his now bloody leather cloak still covering his damaged body.

"Damn it." I shouted as I dragged his limp body and slowly got him into the backseat, beside my gym bag. The duffel bag was filled with my whole life. There were clothes, cash and a few family pictures. And it was all I was keeping from my old life.

Now I had an unconscious man that I covered with my comforter and my cat hissed and spat from the carrier. *Damn it, he's heavy. Oh God he looks like road-kill and smells like death. And why is running around in a freak ice storm? I should have been watching the road. Damn it. He came out of nowhere... I swear he was an animal.*

3

"Please the storm. I need help Jenna. I need you." The man whispered in his deep voice and breathed hard in an injured waking sleep as I finally got him onto the bed. The fire had just made the cabin feel cozy but I felt uneasy with this injured stranger that knew my name. His eyes seemed so familiar but with his bushy beard; I just couldn't remember where I knew this man from. Something just didn't sit right with me about having him here. But my morals always came first and I did hit him with my car.

His face had been partway hidden under his tightly snug leather cloak. But I started unwrapping him to discover a very handsome man with a hard weathered face. The cloak was so tight I had to roll him gently to get him out of the leather while he groaned.

The fire was only burning bright enough for me to see the stranger poorly. My little piece of heaven seemed tarnished as I looked at the damage of his side and realized he was naked under the leather binding. *Frig sakes. Just great I manage to hit a naked, sexy man and now he's dying in my bed. Damn it. Where the frig is the first aid again?* My angry thoughts were set aside as I covered him again with my comforter. The blanket was going to have to be burned because he was losing too much blood. *Great, now he's ruining my favorite blanket. Just frigging great.*

This little place was stocked with enough dried goods, canned preserves, and supplies for years. There was even an underground storage in the backyard that sat nestled on the edge of the mountain far from the world. This cabin was the best gift I had ever been given, even though I hadn't been back to Silver Lake in three years. I remember my Uncle building the storage bunker somewhere on the property for emergencies from severe storms.

The backup power cells and generator was full of enough juice to last one conservative person weeks, possibly even a month before the sun broke through the grey skyline. And I would need to be conservative, now that I had an unwanted visitor and the creatures somewhere off the 3000 acres of protected lands and highway. *This is just great. I'm stuck with a dying man. I have to check his injury but I swear his eyes glowed yellow. Do the Passions have glowing yellow eyes? This storm is supposed to last a week and I'm stuck with the champion of a world bodybuilding contest. No...I'm sure the reporter was adamant about red-eyes. Then what is he? I guess it won't matter soon. If I don't seal up his rippling abs, he's going to bleed to death. I know what I'll do... I'll get one of my Uncle's old silver bracelets to keep paranormal creatures prisoned.*

The big chunky bracelet started frying his tanned skin as soon as it touched his wrist. His face became anguished but his eyes remained closed and his breathing sounded more like a panting dog on a hot summer day.

"I'm going to help you. But I will fight, if you try to kill me. You're losing a lot of blood. I'm going to try and sew it up to stop the bleeding but if it's really bad I'm going to burn it shut. And if you attempt to hurt me; I won't go down without a fight. So don't even think about it." I said as I started applying a warm tea towel to the slash through his torn rippled side.

"You must be joking right? What happened to your left eye? Did someone do that to you?" The stranger said as his eyes were glowing yellow and continued breathing heavy. His face was frowned and he broke out in a feverish sweat.

His body squirmed as I tried to apply pressure hoping that it would stop on its own.

"I don't want to talk about me. You're side…It's still oozing. I know this is hard. But you have to stop moving so much." I said in a shaky voice as my amateur instincts of nursing him back to health was obviously hurting him more.

I knew my inadequateness wasn't what he needed but we both had to endure this if he was going to make it.

"Okay. Just do it quickly and I'll bite the pillow." The strangers pained voice still panted as he shifted his body so his backside was facing me.

His deep wound wrapped around to his back where the most damage had been. *Oh God. It wasn't his front abs. He really is dying. I can see how deep the gash goes. Good Lord he has a glowing moving tattoo of the moon and stars on his butt cheek.*

I grabbed the chef's knife and heated it up in the fire. I pressed hard and smelt the burning flesh and blood while I listened to him howling in agony. My inadequate knife wasn't big enough and I had to repeat the process several times sealing his now imperfect side.

Holding on to the pillow he forced himself to sit up while I wrapped his middle with a thick bandage. The smell of death hung heavy in the air as I eased him back down on the bed and covered him with clean sheets and a dry, thick comforter.

"Jenna, please don't kill me. You don't remember me but I would never hurt you." His voice breathed out the words in a harsh exhale from the pain he endured.

His statuesque body was in a sweat from a feverish illness as he kept his eyes shut with only a murmur of a whisper from his hung, dark voice. His face was roguishly familiar as I searched my memory from where I knew this stranger's likeness. It seemed he could be from a fairytale of my carefree lifetime ago when we were both younger and full of vitality.

But those days were long gone.

My youth had been spent on another that layered my face and body with his fists. And all that remained was someone who could care less about anyone now. There just wasn't anymore love in me to give. Not even to a friend from the past that might have gone through some kind of unholy transformation.

"You might be the person I once knew Fred. But you'll find that life has changed me. Don't expect to get cozy here. You're gone the moment the fever breaks and you're healed." I said as cold as the North wind that blew down from the indigo mountain.

He slowly tossed and turned as I replaced the warm cloth with a cool one to his temple. *He might be gone by early tomorrow if he can't shake this fever. Maybe I should remove the silver so he can heal? Why the hell do I care? I don't even know Fred Dangers anymore. My cat Halloween has been hiding since he got in the cabin and he's a good judge of character. Fred will just have to heal without all his supernatural powers; if he is what I think he is.*

Keeping my pretend nurse hat on I attempted the impossible. I gave him a quick sponge bath because the death smell hung in the air as heavy as every inch of his muscular body. I slipped precariously some comfy pants on him and toppled him with more blankets. He shivered almost violently as he went from sweats to chills, so I made sure the fire stayed a blaze for him.

The fat black cat growled as it hid in the broom storage behind a small built-in cat door. The sound was a weird noise that I hadn't ever heard before and no amount of treats could coax the fur-ball out of the closet.

"Fine Halloween, stay there you coward. You're just like all the other men in my life – weak." I shouted throughout the cabin at the cat expecting a hiss back but only the heavy breathing of his exhales and inhales came.

The whirling noises from the storm outside seemed to blow fierce and made my soul shiver as I watched in amazement the snow coming down. The weather was unusually frigid and winter-like for early autumn.

The large chain was sitting by my closet across from some pictures of the Officers at the Barracks Mills standing beside my Uncle, General Talon Callaghan. In the photo I instantly recognized the man now in my bed and attached the chain to the silver clasp and to the bedpost.

I couldn't stop staring at him sleeping. I had never seen someone dream fight. He wasn't violently thrashing but he was making in-coherent words and then his arm full of stars started glowing. I became so entranced with the glowing stars on his giant forearm that when I looked up and caught him looking at me; it frightened me. His eyes were open and it was like a warm light had turned on inside of him. But as quickly as he had opened his phosphorous eyes they were closed in his fever-driven dreams.

The photos on the walls showed worn uniformed frowning Officer-slaves each sporting a silver bracelet and each looking menacing towards the camera. *So he wasn't one of the Passions. Fred is way more dangerous. He was a Lieutenant and he worked with my Uncle. Maybe he was even the one that killed him? This man is pure, ancient evil and if he lives...I might just have to get the silver bullets out of the back cupboard.*

4

Thinking about Fred's grim face in the photo sent chills down my spine as I topped up the fire. *God I'm exhausted. Thank goodness the couch is comfy. Fred takes up the whole single bed. I wish the bathroom wasn't beside the bed back there. What I need is a nice hot shower to wash away my old life's memories.*

I daydreamed of the shower but cleaned up the blood trail and Fred's bloody cloak throwing everything in the wash machine. Then exhausted from the drive, I didn't stop to think about anything else and dragged myself to the bathroom. With my unwanted houseguest fast asleep and snug in the blankets; I didn't worry about my clear shower curtain or the bathroom being door less.

I just dropped everything and fell in love with the water streaming over all my aches. My body looked like a battlefield of brown and black ugly bruises; so much so that my ribs hurt when the stream touched them. I closed my eyes and just drifted in a dreamless daze of euphoria and pain. I didn't want to seem weak to this blast from the past but I just needed the steam. I needed the heat to hide my tears and hoped the warmth healed my left eye that wasn't swollen anymore but the eye was filled with blood. The small shower mirror reflected how bad I was hurt; and stopping to think about how close it had come to dying was too real. I started sobbing underneath my face cloth. I quickly put the plug-in the tub. *Screw it, I need a bubble bath. Fred's chained up...I deserve this.*

I placed the facecloth over my face and just soaked in the lavender scented bubbles of much needed tender loving care. A flash of a memory came of my mother baking peanut butter cookies and doing tarot cards. The day was warm and the breeze was soft carrying the scent of the jacaranda trees by her balcony. Her gentle face was soft in the sunlight and her brown eyes held a sparkle in them. And that was the first moment in weeks I smiled.

Then in the same moment I gasped as I felt him in the tub grabbing me in his arms and covering my mouth. His bare chest was breathing heavy as he held me tight in his arms and gently moved me to his lap. My eyes went wide in the darkness of the cabin and he held me even tighter against him.

"Jenna, please don't scream. Don't even move. Keep your eyes closed or they will see the light inside you. My eyes are closed too." He whispered in a growl soft into my ear and I obeyed him but my mind was frantic. *What did he mean or they will see the light inside me?*

My hands went up to his arms as I nodded closing my eyes immediately. My hand went to feeling the bracelet first and then two chain links barley holding onto the clasp. The rest of the chain was missing. I gasped again but into his rough hand and he held me tighter against his chest; cradling me into his body as my tears rolled down.

"You mustn't say a word or we're dead. We have to be invisible." Fred whispered fiercely in my ear.

I nodded again as my chest started rising and falling fast. He turned me in his arms and placed my head against his chest.

"Listen to my heart and do not be afraid." He said soothingly as he took his hand off my mouth and caressed my cheek.

His other arm held me tight to his heart and I just sat there listening to his steady rhythm. My breathing slowed to match his as I sat in his embrace on his lap and wrapped my arms around him.

His head rested on my head and I felt his warm breath on my hair giving me this cozy feeling even though we were in peril. In my whole life I had never felt so safe than in this moment of time stopping while in his arms.

His skin had an unusual scent of pines, maples and bacon. *God does he smell lovely. Focus on slowing your heart rate.* My thoughts gave my heart a strict shout and then I tried to match my heart to his failing miserably. I was scared and enamored by his fortitude as he gently touched my sore eye. His touch was as gentle as the softest flower petal and I wondered if he had seen how badly broken I was before he turned the lights off and got into the bathtub with me. As I sat there enveloped in his arms and body; I accidently kept releasing tears and hated myself for being a fair damsel. *I'm stronger than this. Why does his heart speak to mine of kindness? He's a monster and I'm a killer. I have no right to be comforted.*

I tried to pull away with those last thoughts and he brought me in close as we sat in the water that was getting colder and colder. I stayed there with him for hours and we both shivered as the sun's warmth peaked through the window on us.

Faster than an exhale he had carried me to the bed and covered us with blankets. He continued to hold me but rubbed my arms to help bring my waterlogged body back to warmth.

"I'm sorry. I had to make sure they were gone. I'll restart the dying fire and as soon as you are warmed up and I'll make us tea." His rugged voice whispered to me as I started falling asleep from pure physical and mental exhaustion on his bare chest.

I helplessly gave a nod and then passed out to the beating of his heart against my ear.

🌾🌾🌾

5

My face felt hot as I peeled myself from the smooth body I was plastered to. I wiped the drool off the corner of my mouth and wiped the bare skin that was now wet. My eyes went wide as I remembered who this muscular man my naked body was draped over.

"Jenna it's only the afternoon can't we sleep for a few more hours? I prefer to be a nocturnal wolf. Oh and don't worry about the drool; you've been doing that on my breast for hours." Fred's scruffy voice sounded lighthearted as I looked up to his smiling face.

His eyes were shut but he seemed content.

"I was so burnt out. Can you fill me in on what exactly happened yesterday night and why we are both naked?" I said as I looked down to the blanket below my waist and moved it up to my chin trying to create a wall of sheets between us.

"I saw you get into the shower when I heard something coming from outside. At first I thought it was a raccoon. They used to get into your Uncle's garbage all the time and he would bring us here to hunt them. And then torture us and do experiments on us." Fred's growl of a voice turned dark as if he just remembered a suppressed trauma of a memory and then cleared his throat.

"I watched you make a bath and relax. You seemed like you needed a rest since you were pretty beat up. So I was just going to sleep to heal more and then rescue you from drowning in the tub. But I heard the strange scream noise from outside. They had found you. I immediately broke the chain and turned off all the lights in the house. Getting in the tub with you was my only option for our survival." Fred's eyes opened and I saw the yellow glow from before, as his voice had this natural gruff to it but with a soft tone.

We looked into each other's eyes and he cleared his throat.

"I think they are after you for not dying by the roadside with the other cars of people. What do you know about the Passions?"

"Wait a second so you were watching me have a shower and then a bath?" My voice was cracking as my brain digested this piece of information and I instinctively got up using the blankets as a cover and stealing them all off Fred.

Fred looked over and smiled as he was now exposed and quite happy I could see his porn star qualities.

"Good gracious. Put some clothes on Fred. This isn't some cabana. What if they come back?"

"Oh they will eventually." He yawned and stretched his full body on the bed in all his largely endowed glory.

Then slowly he got up and walked over to where I was standing wide eyed at him. I tried to avert my eyes as a blush spread across my face.

"As you can see even with the bracelet I am healing. The scars from where you sealed my wound will eventually fade too." His deep voice said this as his hand went across the side where it looked like he had a huge scar on his right lower abs around to his back.

Even with the discolored pink skin from the burns he was magnificent. I started to look at the ceiling because his mental imagery was locked in my brain as if he had purposefully imprinted himself on me. I listened as his steps came closer stopping in front of me. And I felt him grab both my hands gently bringing them to feel his burnt skin.

"See, you did it. You saved me Jenna."

"Yes I see. But Fred we both need to get dressed." I looked down for a second more and then back up to his breathtaking eyes.

I quickly closed my eyes ignoring what my heart was telling me. Moving slowly he shifted my hands over to his heart and rested his rough hands on top. My eyes opened to his and with his head to the side his blue eyes filled with sorrow as he cleared his throat.

"Jenna you saved my life. You could have let me die and you didn't."

"It's fine." I whispered as I tried to cling to my falling comforter.

"I have done many things in the time I have been on this planet; some good and some not so good. But very few mortals have ever rescued me and only one has ever rescued me from the eternal darkness from where I was going."

"I'm sure I'm not the only one." I said as he pulled me in for a bigger hug which shocked me into releasing the comforter.

He was slowly rocking us back and forth in some sweet dance of gratitude but all I could feel was his nakedness and mine together. I couldn't even focus on what he was saying and I wondered if he was trying to seduce me into taking off his silver bracelet. I immediately pulled away from his sweet embrace and turned around.

"Fred we need to get some clothes on. And if you think you can have me that easy; think again. Even with how handsome you are; I am never going to just bend into your desires or mine." I said as I ignored his lustful proximity to me and started opening the dresser drawers in my desperate need for clothes and space between us.

"You think I'm handsome?" Fred's deep voice sounded surprised and I rolled my eyes. *Of course you're dreamy and handsome. Frig, you could even make movies.*

His arms went around me searching through the dresser drawer too and I froze as I could still feel the heat from his body touching my behind as he leaned over me to get a pair of boxers out.

His heavy hand went to my shoulder and his breathing became heavier on my hair. He started leaning on me and his hand and arms had broken out with beads of sweat. Suddenly he collapsed half on the bed.

I couldn't even scream I was so terrified as I turned around to hear him struggling to breathe again.

"Damn it." I said as he became unconscious and I started helping him back into bed. Tripping over his legs I accidently fell on top of him and my giant bosom fell in his face. *Darn it. Why do I always have to be so clumsy?*

Suddenly I felt his heavy breathing as his hands went to lift my body off him. Quickly he flipped us and his body covered mine completely on the soft cushion of the mattress.

"You know if I wanted to kill you I would have already. All it would take was one slash and this silver bracelet wouldn't stop me." He growled in a low whisper to my ear then collapsed again like a ton of bricks.

"God you are heavy." I said and rolled him back and placed his head on a soft pillow.

I went back and grabbed the comforter and covered him up. His chest and forehead had broken out into little beads of sweat. I checked and discovered he had a really high fever.

He was really ill. His body was fighting some kind of infection. As I touched his cheek it burned my fingers. It was like his skin was on fire. He was that hot. I quickly put a nightie on me, just to get any clothes on and then grabbed a cool facecloth for his forehead. *He's really burning up. I need to cool him down fast.*

My mind started turning to the only thing my mother had taught me about bad fevers. So I started filling the tub with barely warm to cold water and dragged his heavy body over. *What a nightmare.* I sat there in my nightie now drenched holding Fred while he was fighting for his life.

His head lay cradled on my right arm as I kept him half-seated in a hug in the water. One arm held tight around his waist and the other was placing scooped water on his neck and down his strong back. *I am such an idiot. What am I doing? He's the enemy. Why do I care if he lives? Damn it. Why can't I just let him die?*

I felt my heart betraying me as tears escaped down to his fluttering eyelids that opened to mine. His eyes were the deepest pools of blue that I had ever seen. There wasn't any anger in them just a look of mercy as he whispered; "Thank you."

We sat their looking into each other's eyes as I watched his chest inhale heavy and exhale just as hard. His eyes were soft as he tried to stay awake for me but just slept in my arms. Finally after an hour, his fever broke and I helped sturdy him as we both managed to get out of the tub.

"I'm so cold." He whispered and it broke my faint heart.

"Hang on. I'll get you warmed up. Let's grab you some dry clothes and get you back to bed." As I tried to leave he almost fell backwards and we clung to each other to keep upright.

"I…I need your help. I'm too weak." His voice was deep and sad with a hopeless defeated spirit.

"Okay we'll lean on the dresser beside the bed and that way if you feel like you have to fall it will be a soft landing." I tried to sound cheerful but I could even hear the sadness in my voice as we started moving.

He nodded and his whole body started shaking with his teeth chattering in each step. His frowning face was waiting for me to help him undress and I tried to make it painless as his eyes stayed closed. His breathing was harsh as he fell backwards on the bed while I was able to get his shorts to his ankles. With another motion they were off and I moved his blue toes under the covers; covering him up to his chin with layers of blankets.

"Fred just give me a second to get dressed and I will make us some soup to eat. You're probably sicker from starvation by now." I said through chattering teeth as I looked at him already sleeping.

I tossed my wet nightie over my head and faced the dresser opening and closing drawers to find anything that resembled a parka. As my body shivered I rubbed my arms and then looked up to see the shadow on the wall in front of me. Instantly I froze in place with my hands on the dresser drawer facing the darkness of the wall. He was close enough that I could smell his skin and feel the warmth of his body. I watched the large hand with the silver bracelet go by me to help open a drawer.

"We'd both die of hypothermia if I hadn't snapped out of my delirium and slumber; just now. Don't turn around until I'm done dressing and you are." His voice was stern but had a slight shake to it as I felt his breath on my neck.

My hands were frozen to the drawer that was open as I watched his arms around me moving and searching the drawers for clothes. He grabbed a women's flannel shirt and jogging pants for me; and grabbed a pair of men's flannel pants.

As I lifted my arms; I could feel him tenderly tugging an undershirt over my blossoming bosom and then covered me with soft flannel buttoned shirt. The same had happened with the pants he had helped pull up. His actions weren't rushed or heated they were just sincere. His hand touched my bicep giving me a little squeeze as he cleared his throat.

"One second Dove." His voice almost a scruffy growl reminded me of a pirate who may have caught scurvy as it had a shake in it.

My hands went back to waiting on the dresser as his arms went around me and placed back the flannel pants in the drawer and he began to rummage through all the articles. He found a classic white tee and I watched his shadow slip it on over his head. Then he found something that I thought had gone to charity. I don't know how it was still there. But I gasped as he pulled out the wool kilt that had red and green plaid. It went whooshing by my head so fast I couldn't even spit out the objection that was still on its way.

"Um, won't that be itchy? I don't think it's as soft as the flannel." I said as I looked at the drawer being closed in front of me.

He rested his hands on mine and I felt this tingling sensation that couldn't be described. It was like his rough hands held electricity in his fingers; in every touch and my heart started fluttering as my mind was defiantly yelling. *How dare you beat for him treacherous heart. We've sworn off men for eternity, remember?*

6

"There we go. The kilt is warmer by far and I still feel too weak to pull pants up. Although I'm sure you'd help me Dove." He said as he turned me around to face him. My back was against the dresser and my front was facing an iron clad chest through the tight tee he had on and the long kilt. His handsome face looked down onto mine as he fixed a couple of buttons I missed and I stood there watching his intense eyes laser focused on straightening my holes.

"I need you to help me over there. I can't make it on my own." He said as he gave a nod to the bathroom.

That was the one place I absolutely didn't want to be around but I nodded and gulped.

"Okay, we'll have to be careful. I still have to dry up the wet floor." I said as looked at the mess on the floor still and sighed.

"Good. Slow and steady now." He said in his growl of a voice as he placed his hands on my waist and we stepped with each other across the room.

"Don't worry. I don't need you to hold it for me. I can lean." He said with a deep chuckle as I helped prop himself against the door frame.

I left him to his business as I ran back and put wet laundry in the wash machine and dried up the floor. As soon as I heard the flushing sound I turned to face him washing his hands in the small sink.

I heard his faint whisper so low it was like smooth velvet masculine magic that charmed me on a whole other level. "I need your help please."

"Okay don't worry. I got you." I rushed back as he placed his hands on my shoulders to steady himself and we slowly walked back over to the bed.

"Please don't keep me chained up." He whispered from behind my ear and it made my heart beat faster feeling his hot breath on the back of my neck.

His voice was like a starling and it was slathered with an irresistible charm that made my heart an unstoppable flutter. I was suddenly embarrassed as the goosebumps spread across my body making me ache for him. The undeniable feeling I had was evident as the sharp points pushing against the fabric of the front of my shirt. I tried to ignore the forbidden thoughts that were travelling faster than the sound barrier. *He's sick. He might even die. What is the matter with me? Why does his voice make my heart run wild? It has to be werewolf magic. He's using his powers of persuasion over me. Well it won't work.*

We made it over to the bed in turtle speed and he turned me around to face him once more. Slowly, we turned together like a dance so he could be closer to the bed's side as he leaned on me. He even rested his head on my shoulder and I moved my hands from his hips to around him.

Unintentionally we fell onto the bed. His body was under mine as he moved so gracefully with one arm around me I forgot where I was supposed to be. I forgot about everything as he covered us both with blankets and held me in his arms.

I found my ear against his beating heart and his heavy breath in my hair so intoxicating that I started drifting off to sleep once more.

🌾🌾🌾🌾

Early morning the small cabin chilled as I watched my breath in a cloud in front of me. I awoke with his arm slung around my waist and realized I was getting way too comfortable with the heat off his body against me. We were getting to familiar with each other and this had to stop. He may be a man sleeping but he's also a ferocious beast. I carefully moved his arm from around my waist and made sure he was covered. I paused as I watched him snoring sweetly.

His snoring was so enticing that I almost dozed off again too. My body certainly longed to be lovingly held again but I shut those feelings down fast. Instead, I found another chain and re-shackled his silver bracelet to a new twelve foot chain to the bedpost.

It made a loud metal-clank as it clicked breaking the crackling fire noise in the cabin. He didn't move other than the somber up and down of his chest and I grabbed some other blankets and moved over to the couch.

I stocked the fire with logs as I watched the dancing flames and shivered in my new lonely location on the couch.

The storm outside was relentless and viciously blew through the forest in a startling whirling noise that even seemed to shake the small one roomed cabin. There was no light from the window only darkness. Even though it was early morning you couldn't hear any sweetness of the little song birds that I truly missed. In fact I bet no manner of creature was out in this weather.

The wind roared and I held my blankets tighter up to my chin. The roaring sometimes sounded like howling and I wondered if the wolves might break down the door at any time and rescue their friend.

As the roaring continued, I drifted off and snuggled deep in the comfort of the tin roof that was still overhead while the fire blazed on through the chilled air of the cabin.

🌱🌱🌱🌱

7

The floor boards creaked and my eyes fluttered open to the sound coming from the kitchen behind me. I turned to the window and caught my breath in my throat at the glowing yellow eyes completely focused on me in the partial darkness.

Swirls of white snowflakes swam past the window as the roaring continued outside but the noise and poor visibility of the storm wasn't what gave me chills as I looked into the fierce eyes past my toes and past the end of the couch at the small table. He never broke our gaze even as I rubbed the sleet and crust out of my eyes from a thousand unrealized dreams.

Quicker than I could open my mouth he was up and headed towards me with two things in his hands. My vision was blurred as he approached with heavy footsteps but my mind was panicked. *He was free about the cabin again. I wonder for how long? Stupid chains; I should have checked to make sure they were silver. I wonder if he is going to kill me now.*

Suddenly a heavenly coffee aroma filled my nostrils and I could smell the freshly ground beans with a hint of lavender. It was some fancy coffee my Uncle was addicted to before the world went to hell. I suddenly wondered if the financial system hadn't crashed; if I would have been a multi-millionaire off the coffee stock he owned. Then my focus and vision became clearer as a mug was being handed to me and I grabbed it clinging to the foreshadowed deliciousness and the extra warmth it would bring.

I immediately sat up and moved my legs beside me which in-avertedly gave him an opening invitation to sit with me in front of the fire. He didn't pause and sat quicker than an objection could come from my dry lips.

"Thank you but…"

"But you thought you could contain me. You can't. The chains aren't silver. The clasp is and it does hurt but I can get used to the pain. My name is Frederik Dangers. But everyone calls me Fred. We have met a very long time ago. Time moves quickly and covers the fun times of youth only to leave this new apocalyptic future. But it was a different world back then for both of us." His deep voice sounded like black velvet; smooth and soft and full of mysteriousness.

"Fred I remember you. You were that hard-ass camp counselor that used to make us do squats and pushups. So why did you stay?" I said as I loved every moment of this decadent, fresh indulgence but tried not to sound happy that he had given me such pleasure that I had forgotten existed.

"Why? Why am I still here? I have morals. It's not the storm that is keeping me here or this charming shiny bracelet eating away at the flesh on my wrist. You saved my life and I am in debt to you until I fulfil my life debt. I am your humble servant, your bodyguard, and maybe even your chef." His sultry voice was so sexy I remembered briefly his naked body against mine and my breath escaped my lips in a sigh.

"Wait. What? You can't stay here. Consider your debt paid." I said and tore my eyes away from the larger than life monster under his kilt as he caught me stealing glances.

"So you'll free me?" He whispered so charming that my heart skipped but I remained cool.

"I can't remove the bracelet. You are too dangerous. I can't let you go be your natural self in the wilderness and hurt any unsuspecting humans that come across your wrath."

"Why can't you set me free?"

"Because you're a monster and the world has enough killers out there. And I know the legends are true. Each month you need to taste blood as punishment from the Gods." I said harshly and focused on my mug.

"So you would free me, but not really. I can't really be myself. Would you have me defenseless in the wilderness?" He spoke in a growl but it sounded as if he was wounded.

"I'm alone in this world and I'm okay." I said and took a sip without looking into his eyes that I could feel studying me.

"Listen you aren't alone and either am I. You can't keep me contained forever. Why are you so afraid of my true form?" His scruffy voice asked harshly but still held a hint of sadness.

"Because werewolves kill people just as much as the Passions do. There are so many senseless killings in this world and because of what? A macho power trip over the light of the full moon. No Fred. I will never set you free. You can be just as normal as I am and the rest of all the highest society and not a lower-class form. A nice and normal part of the higher race of non-killers and non-animalistic butchers."

"Are you really so delusional as to believe that humans are superior or that humans don't kill other humans? The war within the human race has been fighting since existence. I may have killed for freedom and for survival but I have never hunted out of sadism. You call me a monster yet here I am speaking to you as a man. I'm not using my God given charms or any werewolf magic tricks. In fact I don't need magic to kill you or for my pack to kill you. My wrist may be held back because of my new silver jewelry but my strong hands still work. If I wanted you dead you wouldn't be drinking that coffee. I would have done it while you slept and showed you mercy. But what you don't realize about werewolves we are not the same as the Passions and the humans that rule the world." He spoke so sincere I was shocked and amazed and hanging off all of the pure sounds of his voice.

He cleared his throat and sipped some of his mug.

"I just want the same thing you do Jenna. I just want peace and to live. This prison you keep me in will slow my healing down and keep me from transforming but eventually I will break free of this shackle. What is really keeping me here is not the prison but the caring heart that saved mine." His voice was calm and still charmed the pants off me but my face grew hot.

"You know nothing of what I want. You are nothing but a beast and if I had enough brains in my head, I would have aimed when I hit you with my car. Then I wouldn't be stuck smelling wet dog throughout the cabin and an unwanted repayment."

"Why do you hate me so much Jenna? What have I or the Blue Moon Society ever done to you?"

"My Uncle ran the Barracks Mills. He was General Talon Callaghan. He hated you monsters and captured you one by one. He captured your power for his fist in his great army of justice. With his control you were given the power to rule the unworthy criminals of society. He gave you purpose and direction and you destroyed him for it. My whole family has hated your kind for centuries." I said harshly and glared at his beautiful sparkling blue eyes.

"But what is it that you really hate? Or is it fear? Fear that you can't control the magic in the world? Fear of anything different than you? I am nothing like the Passions whose name is a complete contradiction of the soul they lack. Those creatures are merciless beings that prey on anything that isn't to their liking. They are born from the bowels of the red Earth and centuries of blood spilt over the rich soil by humans against humans. The Earth arose to defeat you. Not my kind. The red eyes are all the doom you have brought upon yourselves in your quest for power and glory. The true monsters have always been the uncaring beings that try to control everyone's freedom." He said in a growl with such force in his voice it brought my eyes to his.

"Do you even know how many beings your Uncle has enslaved? Monster or human? Do you know how many he has murdered to keep productivity and the status quo? All of the thousands of innocents he has slain? Or how many he has defiled with his body? You don't. But I was in the Barracks Mills. You have no idea how many people I was forced to devour because of his rage. But I know." His voice held the growl but spoke softer.

"You are nothing but a liar and you can sleep on the floor like the dog you are. You should thank me for not kicking you out in this storm and letting you freeze to death. Because right now that's the only thing I want." I said and tears welled up.

"Fine my little Dove. Have it any way you want. But heed this warning. When I am fully healed and have repaid my debt of '*a life for a life*', I will remember your compassion or lack of. And it will be what saves your soul from my packs vengeance or immortal gift. It's your choice. But I still offer my hand to yours in servitude until my debt is repaid." He looked into the fire and it looked like his eyes had dancing flames in them from the magnitude of his power.

His voice had been a steady defiance and I uneased in what I had said to him. He was right about my Uncle even when I was young he had seemed dangerous the way he spoke through a snakes hiss and carried a knife in his boot. But I couldn't take it back and I didn't want to believe his steady voice full of a harsh unflinching truth. So I continued to watch the flames dance and keep my mind's ignorance. It was the only thing I had left. *What does this mean if my family has been the bad guys? No, I can't think like that. But here he is unchained and I haven't heard any deception in his voice. This has to be a trick. Maybe he poisoned me?*

I pulled the blanket closer to me and shuddered as the chill grew between us. He got up and gently tugged my mug convincingly from my hand and I made the mistake of looking up into his eyes. His eyes were as soft as the flannel that hugged my skin but carried all the sadness you see in truly broken and lonely people. I know this because I had that same look of despair.

When his finger touched mine to grab the mug an electrical current zapped us. I flinched but he remained calm.

My eyes followed him to the kitchen. There was something about Fred. I had always known there was this mysterious feeling between us. But I didn't believe in destiny or fate. I barely believed in werewolves until I seen his eyes glowing. My Uncle always told us stories but he was nothing like my Uncle's description.

In fact Fred was the furthest from even being the drill sergeant camp counselor he used to be. His demeanor was much more kinder than I remembered.

8

This unexplainable feeling came over me while I watched him refill our mugs. This was the first time a man had ever done anything for me. He came back just as quickly; carefully handing me the filled pottery mug and placed his hand around mine to make sure I had it. I made the mistake of looking into his eyes again as we got zapped by that magic that surrounded his presence.

His gaze met mine with just as much intensity and I realized I was in the presence of something I had never known ever. Fred was kind. And it broke a small piece of my armor and I turned away from that light in his eyes. He had this perfect sparkle that lit up like I was some kind of treasure he'd just found. I had never seen anyone look at me like that before and it hurt knowing I was abused for years by a lesser man. And that's what I thought real love was.

He sat back beside me on the couch this time closer and I wondered if it was my fluttering heart that gave me away or if it was the small teardrop I quickly wiped away. In truth I wanted to be stronger than him and I wanted to hate him. But I just couldn't; something in my soul flew to his whenever he was near. My whole being knew who he was and still my pig-headed mind wanted to be free. My spirit longed to be with his running through some meadow. In one glance of those deep blue eyes I had forgotten any malice or guilty charges against his spirit. My heart wanted that freedom just as bad as his.

When he tore away from our soul binding stare; I could feel the air between us change and in his absence my teeth chattered. I snuggled my blanket up to my chin. Clinging to the heat from my replenished mug; I took an unladylike long slurp. *Good, I hope he likes refined ladies. That should stop the chemistry between us.*

From the dark of the day I could hear his slurping sounds echoing through the cabin matching mine. *Damn it. How can he even slurp cute?*

I looked back over to him now even closer on the couch and his hand rested on my feet. I took a nice long slurp and closed my eyes enjoying this pot of gold.

"So what can I do for you my little Dove?"

"Everything." I said and set my cup down precariously on the little table.

I was uncontrollable tired and curled up falling asleep on the arm of the couch. My need for a nap beat any unresolved need to argue from our past discussion.

"What's going on? Jenna? Jenna? Hang on Jenna. Just listen to the sound of my voice and come back to me. Please Jenna. Please come back." I heard the concern in his scruffy voice.

⁂⁂⁂

Slowly my eyes fluttered open and I groaned as I clutched my stomach. My face felt like it had been plastered to his muscular chest for hours because I seemed to be used to listening to the strange rhythm of his heart.

"There you go. It's okay, I'm here for you. I'm here." His voice was deep and soothing.

My stomach churned as I gripped his bare chest hugging him vicariously with my arms. It was like instinctively if I could capture the warmth of his skin against mine I could harness the power to heal my illness and wounded soul. My face was against his chest and I was lying on top of him with a million blankets over my back. I could feel his chest rise and fall and his warm breath down in my hair. I could feel something even larger that had woken up just when I had and I shifted my body over as I placed my hand underneath the blanket. He gasped as I did and it sobered us up completely as it throbbed against the heat of the inside of my legs.

"Wait a minute Fred, why are we in bed? And why are we naked again?" I said as I pulled my hand and legs back and rolled off him to his side in shock.

"You caught the death-flu just like I had when you hit me with the car." He said in a whisper into my hair and I realized I still clung to his warmth unabashedly and my arms weren't letting him go.

"I had to get your fever down just like you helped me." His voice was a soft growl and my whole body felt like I couldn't let him go.

The electricity between us was too addictive and even though I had moved to his side; the pulsating heat from underneath the sheets was undeniable.

"But we were clothed Fred. Uuugghh, seriously I feel like crap. I can't deal with this." I lied as I tried to catch my breath but still held him tight.

"I can assure you nothing has happened. You were shivering so violently after the fever; I had to try and warm you up. You are still very ill. I...I almost thought...I lost you." Fred's scruffy voice was so deep but went an octave higher with that last remark.

Fred was a very muscular fellow but completely knocked the stereotype of macho, muscular-alpha out of the window with that last comment. *I heard it. The sensitivity in his tone. I must have almost died and he actually saved me again.*

"Uuugghh...I feel like I'm dying." I said as it took all my strength to turn completely away from him and clutched my stomach grasping to end the pain.

"Easy now, I made us some stew. I'll fetch it for you Dove." He said as he flicked on the lamp and his beautiful body-builder loveliness walked across the room.

"Jeeze Fred get some clothes on. You'll scare the deer outside." I said as he took my breath away.

"Ha. Don't flatter me. I know I'm nothing like my twin brother Darion. Besides those deer were eaten days ago. I just need to find my...Oh there it is." He sounded happy as if he found pirate booty across the room and I watched him wrap the kilt around his muscular buttocks. *God he looks like an underwear model. Why is there a bedside mirror right here? Damn it, he just turned and flashed me before he got that plaid secure. Frig...Woof. Damn it he saw me watching him.*

"Seriously Fred a quilt? What's up with that? There are all kinds of men's clothes in here. What's with the plaid obsession?" I said as I turned around to watch what he was doing while clutching the blankets up to my chin.

"I don't have a plaid obsession. You do. I remember when my clan fondly used to be fashionable in kilts and axes. Times were different back then. We had ravaged and pillaged so much we had to cross the sea. Our mighty Viking leader Oden Wolfinshire founded this forest and what you know as Wolfinshire City. Our mighty Blue Moon Clan was unstoppable. We were here long before the magic became visible. I was a fierce warrior back then. The mere look into my eyes could drop men to their knees begging for my mercy. I could slay three men at once, yielding my axe in one blow. In fact, before the curse we were all a fearless, fearsome tribe of Vikings. We were merciless and unyielding just as much as the Passions. Even more so I think. What a vengeful time of blood and carnage. It took us a millennium to escape and redeem ourselves. But that is another story for another time." Fred spoke full of zest of the life he left in the past and the passion in his voice was addictive.

He frowned as he looked out the window and I saw his reflection deep in thought.

My stomach broke the sound of the storm still raging but my eyes were on Fred now in pure fascination. He was something straight out of my mom's forbidden bedtime stories. Too devilishly handsome to be human maybe that was the problem. He made it too easy to forget he was a horrific monster on the inside because his outside wrapping paper was too pretty. *God I feel so sick. I hate myself for looking at those rippling abs. Even his voice sounds like some sexy pirate. Woof.*

I watched him scandalously as he gently stirred a pot and swayed the fabric back and forth as he hummed to himself.

All I could see was the kilt swish to and fro. And my mind tried to hold decent thoughts of the sexy man before me who was bringing me dinner in bed. But my drifting thoughts couldn't help but notice his biceps flex as he walked towards the bed. And each pectoral muscle that seemed to move in some kind of happy bounce back and forth to the hum of his sexy voice.

Placing the bowls beside the night side table he placed his forearm on my temple to check my temperature and then walked back to grab the small chair. He moved his chair as close to me as possible. It was so close I thought maybe I was going to be eating out of his lap pleasurably; but my thoughts varied and I realized the delusions from the sickness.

Random thoughts popped into my head like remembering Fred from summer camp at Silver Lake. It was never that Fred was unattractive he always had been. He just seemed so unattainable. He was so good looking we were afraid to even speak to him. The guys in camp were just afraid of him in general. Whenever someone acted out, Fred made sure we were back in tune to the activities of the day; including the daily punishment of squats and pushups from hell.

The smell of spices and a beef broth filled the air in a wondrous aroma. But I blew my nose unladylike again breaking the euphoria of a home cooked meal. *God am I sick.*

"Okay Dove, let's try a little at a time shall we?" His sultry voice could cut butter and I hung on each syllable.

"You're gonna try and spoon feed me?" I asked out of breath from even breathing.

"I watched you barely able to lift that tissue to your nostril. You're pretty weak my Dove. So…" His growl was soft as I looked into his dreamy blue eyes.

"I can do it." I said defiantly and tried to lift my head up but collapsed.

I was so exhausted but I gave just enough energy to give Fred an angry look for a fraction of a second. *I'll show you. I'm tough.*

His eyes remained unchanged and just as soft as a kitten. And now I wondered if he really was this fierce monster I had always heard from legends or if actually he was something else completely void of anger. The lights started flickering with the storm suddenly like it was really picking up out there.

"I think we might have to conserve the energy in here. The backup generator can only hold so much. It's not like we're gunna see the sun for a few." Fred was speaking and it was the first time he hadn't covered his ancient accent from escaping.

I wondered if he hid it, just like everything else in his world. If I didn't know better of what kind of devil he was; I would think I was talking to a regular guy. I could even see a warm glow of compassion in his eyes as he propped me up with some pillows and threw a nightie over my head. He even helped my arms through the sleeveless spaghetti straps.

I looked at the gown and tears welled up in my eyes. This had been my Aunt's favorite. It was plain but had a crescent of daisies over the heart and seeing it brought memories of her when she was very ill and dying.

I turned away from Fred but the mirror caught my sadness and Fred was looking just as sad. It seemed that I had the same problem as my very late Uncle. I couldn't let go. And that was why this cabin was full of old memories; good and bad. The cotton felt new and soft. It was like the fabric had captured her essence of sunshine and lavender from the dried flowers in the drawers.

"It's okay Dove." Fred said as he patted my arm softly.

I looked back at him completely giving up the daggers that were trying to slay him a moment before and melted through my disguise as I surrendered. Suddenly the bowl was sitting with the other one on the bedside table and his arms were around me.

"We will go slowly okay and if you need me to rush you to the loo all you do is tap my hand twice. Okay my Darling." He said in his scruffy voice and made sure I was steady against some pillows.

As soon as he spoon fed me I started to fall in love with his stew. It had potatoes, carrots, and even onions. *God I hate onions. But this is just so good.*

My body felt so drained and more than that my ego hurt. A stranger from the past was taking care of me. I had to rely on his care to even eat or get dressed. It was embarrassing enough that I took care of him and now he was taking care of me. But with each delicious spoonful my ego deflated. I didn't want to seem piggish but it was so addictive. Hands down the best stew I ever had. I bit down on something round and popped it like a grape as the weirdest flavored juice filled my mouth. It was like there was a utopia on my tongue. The oozing juices tasted extraordinary. The round object was filled with a spicy liquid that I couldn't put my finger on. I could definitely taste a hint of nutmeg and cardamom. *This is so delightful. Man is this ever good.*

"This is so good. I have never tasted anything quite like it. That last bite was especially delicious. Thank you Fred. All this goodness is really making my stomach feel better." I said and he dabbed my mouth with a napkin.

"That's great. I'm glad you like the stew. This recipe has been in the family for centuries. What you just ate is a little known delicacy and there are only ever two in the whole pot." Fred sounded excited talking about the stew I felt like he adored it, just as much as my taste buds did.

With each bite I had been closing my eyes enjoying the flavors and didn't have my eyes open until I heard him speak about the stew.

Then my eyes opened into his I could see him smiling and he was simply radiant. My heart fluttered wildly as I looked into his magmatic eyes and he smiled warmly at me.

9

Before I knew it I had managed to take the bowl from Fred and shamelessly slurped the stew devouring it completely. This stew really was the most mouthwatering dish I had ever had the pleasure to eat. Fred in that moment had finished his bowl in no more than one heartbeat after I had finished. It was like we were in some professional eating contest and he was the King. He cleared his throat and I dreamily looked at his fanged smile.

"Should I get you more rabbit stew? You really enjoyed that eyeball faster than I ate mine." His voice was as smooth as a phone sex operator but my mouth gaped open and I looked aghast at my empty bowl.

His voice was sincere but my mind yelped as did my rich, pampered soul.

"What did you feed me?" My voice waivered irrationally.

"Rabbit Stew; it's been a family recipe for centuries if not longer." Fred's sexy pirate voice was light hearted but I shifted my eyes from my bowl to his gaze.

His eyes sparkled with this dazzle I wish I had. But my ego couldn't get over that I just ate some Viking recipe that might give me a case of botulism.

"I need a bowl. I think I'm going to puke."

"Oh Dovey this stew is too hearty to waste. I doubt your stomach will let all that nourishment go. Besides it'll help keep you warm with all the chest hair you'll grow." His voice was charming as he chuckled in a growl but I was still appalled.

"What? Seriously Fred, never cook that recipe again." I said and pouted.

"Oh once you have it, you'll need it. In fact you'll beg me to cook that recipe for you again. Your stomach and body will ache for it." He laid the charm on thick and my ego broke into a grin across my face with widening blush.

"I don't think we are living in the same world Fred. I think I would rather die than eat that stew ever again." I teased and moved the pillows so I could lie back down and I felt him move the blankets tucking them up to my chin for warmth. *God was that stew good. Why couldn't I just say that? I mean its rabbit. I'm too rich to enjoy rabbit aren't I? God was that ever good. I can't ever talk to anyone about what I enjoyed so much. Secretly, how the round object oozed out was like the center of a chocolate filled with melted goodness. I hope I didn't hurt his feelings.*

My thoughts drifted as I heard Fred whistling a medley over water sloshing and dishes chiming. Just before I was completely out I felt the blankets shift and strong warm arms wrapped around my body in the sweetest embrace. I immediately turned to him and held him back.

"Thank you Fred. That stew was amazing." I whispered as I fell asleep placing my head on his bare chest whose heart beat fierce against my ear. It was like I belonged in his arms and I couldn't remember what it felt like before.

❋❋❋❋

His side of the bed was empty as my hand reached and only found the rest of the blankets. I woke up feeling a hundred percent better like I could run a marathon. *What was in that stew? Perhaps werewolf magic?*

I sat up and moved slowly to the washroom but the more I moved the better I felt. Completely forgetting about Fred's whereabouts I had what could only be described as the best shower of my life. Even the scent of cucumber from the shampoo felt invigorating and brought me back from the grave. I slathered the artisan strawberry soap all over, making giant suds all over my sore body. *God does the shower ever make my soul feel alive this morning.*

I suddenly froze as I opened my eyes to glowing yellow eyes through the clear curtain.

"Jenna I'm leaving towels for you and I will be back shortly from getting wood." His growled voice seemed out-of-breath and huskier than normal.

But before I could even say a word he was gone with his candle lit eyes and I heard the door to the cabin bang shut.

I grabbed the towels from the rack and wrapped my hair and then my body. The cabin was so nice and toasty and I could smell fresh coffee which I couldn't wait to enjoy.

The heat from the cabin was so nice that removing my towel to get clothes on wasn't freezing but freeing. It was just me and no wild animal man to apologize to. I was the King of my castle again and he was outside; so I strutted to the dresser carefree and then waded through clothes.

"Excuse me Jenna." His deep voice came from across the room.

"Eeeek, Fred don't look at me. I'm naked." I said as I tried to cover myself with my hands.

"Actually you have underwear on, which is not naked at all. And I have seen you a lot more naked than that." His sexy voice was charming and sweet but I was starting to freeze.

"Get out Fred. Get out." I said holding my ground.

"Okay I just needed my toque and mittens it's freezing outside without my warm fur."

"Okay just grab them and get out." I said while trying to grab a pillow to hide.

"Oh here they are." Fred said more softly as he took steps towards me and reached by my arm to grab the pair of mittens and toque on the dresser while I held my breath and time stopped.

Our eyes were locked in some enticing trance and my heart was skipping.

10

His eyes were such a fierce blue that even in what little light there was from the bathroom; I could feel a pull in his intense gaze. I stood there lost in a sweet space where the rules of time didn't apply. The clocks hands weren't ticking on the wall as I stood there in the thick wilderness of his deep blue oceans.

My pillow suddenly slipped from my hands and I gasped but he caught it instantly as our eyes never left each other's. His eyes seemed to be attached to mine as if some invisible silver chain had secured us together in this small moment and our hands touched with some electrical feeling as he passed the plush pillow.

Daringly, he leaned in and kissed my cheek with the same electrical shock against my skin and I closed my eyes. Suddenly, I was swept away to standing in a meadow full of sunflowers. The sun was warm against my skin. It was such a vivid fantasy that I felt my soul shaken as my reality changed. My hand went instantly up in reaction and gave his hand a soft squeeze.

"Okay I'll see you soon." I whispered and shivered as he kissed my cheek again; leaving me to feel the winter in his absence. My hand went back to my face and tried to trace the lingering warmth from his luscious lips.

Snapping back from the experience I just had was impossible. My fingers seemed to lack the enthusiasm of getting buttons done up properly on my flannel shirt. *What was it about Fred? It's like I can feel a small rush from his steady heartbeat whenever he holds me. I can't place this feeling because I have never had this with anyone. But one thing is certain I hate the lack of control he makes my reckless heart feel.*

As I slipped on my socks the fire seemed alive and full of sparks. Everything was nice and cozy and it really got under my skin. The aroma in the air smelt like the smoky fire and maple flavored bacon all through the cabin.

Walking to the kitchen, I noticed how neat and tidy everything was and the covered plate with a mug. A similar mug of coffee sat across from it and the table was set with yellow roses in an orange vase in the center. The closer I got the more my nostrils took in the fresh smell of coffee first brewed. *He made coffee and breakfast. Damn it. I really hate that guy...God is this hot coffee ever good and the bacon. Heaven. I have died and went to Heaven, which is the only explanation for this. Damn it, he put strawberry jam on my toast. God I hate him.*

Every bite was amazing the omelet was the essence of perfection with a mixture of spices. My mouth really was having a party and my dull brain was not invited or my poor attitude. Everything was too scrumptious for words. And I guiltily ravaged my plate, wolfing everything down. It was like I had never had anything so desirable in my life. A breakfast only made by werewolf magic I presumed. The kind to entice and keep you forever locked in their domain. *He can't win my heart with food. No matter how damn good this is. God even the flowers are beautiful. Nope. I've made up my mind. He's a werewolf and still a monster. He's still the enemy and he's mine forever. I will never set him free.*

Unladylike I let a small amount of juice from the bacon escape from the corner of my greedy mouth. Greed wasn't even the proper word…contemptuous and disastrous; fit better. As I ate I was still trying to reason with myself how to hate him even after all the wonderful things he had done for me. I may have saved his life but he was actually taking care of me and technically he had already paid the debt back twice now. I'm positive I wouldn't have made it from the death-flu that was plaguing our grand Earth reset.

Fred burst through the door slamming it quickly. His arm was slashed and blood was coming through his jacket. The wide-eyed expression mirrored my own. His chest heaved up and down like he had been running.

"I don't know if you realize that there is a root cellar to this cabin. It was a smaller bunker in case of severe storms. We need to move there quickly. Gather any extra blankets you can carry. I'll explain later. We have to leave here now." Fred's usually scruffy calm voice sounded alarmed and made me get up and run to the bed to grab blankets.

Then I ran to the closet gathering extra emergency blankets. I slipped over my head the shoelace necklace of the key to Fred's silver bracelet and then ran to the door where he waited for me.

I pulled on my jacket and boots; and bundled up with mittens fearing the worst. I could hear the wind roaring through the snow falling outside the window. I stopped dead in my tracks as I heard something else through the bustling trees branches. The distinct eerie screaming sound through the woods was getting louder and louder as the noise came closer and closer.

Fred grabbed my hand and pulled me outside through the snow to the small door on the back of the property. It had been cleared off to open but was easily covered back up from the snow falling so heavy. The weather wasn't normal for now early October. *I wouldn't have thought in a million years I would see snow days before Thanksgiving.* That thought escaped as I thought I seen a flock of wild turkeys run past us into the woods.

The large metal door opened with a metal creak as he forced me to climb the stairs leading into the darkness. This was the one place I never visited after it was constructed or after my Aunt and Uncle's death. I had only remembered the excavator digging out the bunker and the cement foundation being poured. But I was always forbidden to enter and I hesitated to take the first step as Fred pushed me to go inside.

"I have to go back. Stay in here and go to the middle part of the bunker where the small table is. There is a cord over the table to turn the light on. If you reach up you'll find it." Fred shouted over the screaming noises and then left me closing the door securely.

A moment later, the metal door swung open and piles of wood were placed on the large landing of the first step. I could hear the creepy screaming closer than before as he pulled the heavy metal against the strong winds. Then the door closed firmly and I heard the metal bolts in an interlocking system that made the vault of a bank sound weak.

Fred grabbed my hand and we walked down the rest of the long curvy stairwell. Everything my Uncle had created was grand and this wasn't an exception. But this place gave me chills for no reason other than my Uncle's eccentricity. I remembered this place gave abandoned attics of haunted castles look like Shangri-La. This place was definitely scary including walking through the void to get to the first light switch.

The walls had round extrusions that popped out; cold and textured. There were indents and sharp pieces but there were intricate details in each bump on the wall. I could feel the shape of a star carved in each one. My fingers and hands followed each small round shape down the wall. There were rows and rows of these shapes in the wall. *What an interesting decoration. There must be hundreds. I wonder if this was decorated by my Aunt who loved different textures and double stitching in decorations.*

"We only have a three day supply down here. Hopefully that is enough time for the storm to stop and then we can make a break for it to the mountains and my pack." His growled voice seemed strained.

"Where is the light switch?"

"We have to use it sparingly or they will find us and kill us. One of the Passions was a giant redwood and it caught me splitting wood. I killed him but he screamed for the others. We are dead if we don't hide right now. Or you could free me from my restraint and I can save us both." Fred's growled voice sounded hopeful.

"Not a chance. What would stop you from leaving me defenseless in this place? Fred we need to find some other kind of light than your eyes." My voice was shrill and sarcastic not an opportune time to be making jokes but I was sure Fred could feel my fear as I squeezed his hand tighter.

"Fine. Into the darkness we go." Fred's voice was not trembling and his calm unnerved me as my heart panicked.

While he held my hand tight, my other hand felt the round bumps on the wall. With each step we took down the stairwell, the screaming and wailing outside started to get smaller and smaller until it was no more than a whisper as we reached the smooth ground.

Fred and I walked for some distance as he stopped and the light went on with a loud clicking sound.

My mouth gasped at the sight.

The walls and ceiling; that I thought might be decaying because of the holes and sharp pieces were something shocking and sinister. I was looking at hundreds, if not thousands of werewolf skulls embedded from floor to ceiling. This wasn't just a bunker. This was some sort of crypt. And each skull had delicate carvings of some ancient language detailed into the bone. All had a six-pointed star in the center of the forehead with astral constellations and moon phases on the cheekbones and chin. Some even had intricate detail carved on their sharp canines in the same foreign language.

"I…I…" I stuttered to put to words the horror I was viewing with dread and distaste. Especially as I looked on and seen very small skulls and very large ones.

"I knew you didn't know about this place. The first night I met you on the road. I was coming here for a quick shelter from the storm since I knew your Uncle was dead. I was ready to kill you for the sins of your relatives, if I smelt that evil in your blood. But you had this innocence about your beaten beauty and I knew I could trust you." Fred cleared his dry throat and I thought I heard heartbreak in the tone as his eyes glowed in viewing the skulls.

"Your family has been hunting mine since we came over on our long ship." He whispered.

"You were going to kill me?" I gasped.

"I was going to survive at all costs. There was no way my head was going to be added to your trophy wall and then I caught the death-flu sweeping the world." His growled voice seemed somber.

"I never knew about this…the extent. I never knew how far the blood feud went." I said still in shock as I looked around the room and tears welled up in my eyes as I seen tiny skulls.

"I know. Your eyes spoke to me when the room was illuminated." Fred's voice became a whisper as he gently caressed a skull on the wall.

His fingers rubbed delicately the star and carving and it glowed in response. Then as if by magic all the skulls and ancient language became a fluorescent indigo.

My eyes went wider as small tears escaped the corners. It was *'hauntingly beautiful.'* And it was the first time that phrase ever struck a chord of a sorrow filled tempo playing on my sinking heart.

I loved my Uncle but had never known the true crimes of his internal war with magical creatures he felt that didn't shine in God's likeness. I had remembered him giving me personal sermons and thinking he was crazy because werewolves weren't real.

But this was real. And I didn't know this sadistic side of my Uncle or family. I left home at eighteen following my heart to the city and a boy. And as soon as I left I was an outcast to everyone, except my Aunt. I wondered if she had known or if she was too sick to know.

This was a horrible realization and I sat down at the table. My Uncle had tried to convince me that werewolves were monsters. I looked over to Fred who was whispering and kissing a few of the skulls and I wondered if all the fallen had been just as compassionate as him.

If they were half as kind and as peaceful as Fred, than everything I knew was wrong. *How do you apologize for all the sins of your bloodline? Is there any hope of redemption or forgiveness for me? If not, can I ever hope to be free from this nightmare of truth?*

11

I wiped my eyes quickly and looked on the floor to hide my wet face. I hated crying because I had no right to be sorrowful. This was his beautiful family that my ugly family had murdered. They were murdered just because they didn't fit into a perfect box that society had created. Anything magical had been blasphemous and against the bible. But he was just as special as an eighth wonder of the world and I looked over to him still kissing the skulls that lit up with each gift of love.

His sweet murmurs and deep voice echoed the room like a soothing lullaby. When his hand was up I noticed his sleeve expose the white of his wrist bone from the silver clasp moving down his arm burning and rotting his flesh every time it rested on his skin.

I quickly turned away from the silver shimmering in the light. It was the bracelet I had placed on him and I felt a lump get stuck in my throat as some more tears escaped.

All of the skulls with their magic alive stopped glowing and I looked up to see Fred lying down on the small single cot completely turned away from me.

"Fred can I make you a tea?" I whispered over to him.

"No Jenna. I do not want a tea. The sooner we leave this place of pain the better." His voice almost seemed like a snarl as he didn't look at me.

"You with your fancy coffee and fine silks that you hide away with all the silver spoons of the blood fortune you were born with. And my good fortune and my destiny you keep me from. But you can't ever steal that from me. My fortune is alive and well running through the wilderness. It is the inextinguishable flame that will burn even after I am gone regardless. So continue to keep me as your prisoner for the debt I am willingly paying. But don't you dare lick my wounds and tell me you're sorry. Your tears fall into the vastness of the hollow pit in the floor; right along with all the other bowel movements of despair. I neither weep nor bring comfort to thee right now. Leave me be." His pirate voice was sultry and harsh and made me silent cry.

"I don't understand how you could hate me this much. I was an Officer at the Barracks Mills and a slave. I have done many dark deeds to be free and to free others. But that is my past. I am not my past and neither are you. Can't you unshackle me and set my soul free? We both have a chance to be completely free from our history. Can't you see that?" His deep voice almost whispered this directly to my heart as I heard his spirit call to mine.

I stayed at the table and clutched my teacup for warmth looking at the teabag sink to the bottom of the cup; along with my heart. I could hear booming up above and weird screaming noises but remained silent.

Letting tears escape down my face on my arm. *I'm so sorry Fred. I'm sorry.* My thoughts became cloudy as I turned off the light and fell asleep gripping my teacup with all the strength I could muster from a shattered heart.

⁂

In the middle of a dreamless dream of an eternity of sadness, came a whisper of hope to my despaired heart. I was being carried by his big, warm arms. Strong arms delicately placed me on the bed and removed my outer clothes. Then I was being wrapped with blankets as I felt a kiss on my cheek.

⁂

I awoke to loud bangs from above and thought the gruesome ceiling might collapse.

"Fred." I whispered but couldn't reach for him in the dark.

"Fred where are you?" I whispered again as I could hear crashing from above.

I got up extending my arms in the dark walking blindly towards the table and stubbed my foot on one of the legs. *Ouch, did I ever hurt my big toe. Where the hell is Fred?*

Reaching up I found the cord and pulled hard to illuminate the room. The click seemed even louder as the booming from above became distant for a moment before returning. I could now hear the terrifying screaming sound from before and knew the Passions had to be above me. Looking around I noticed Fred was missing. *He left me. I guess it was too much for him. I was too much. Well he was right. I wish I could be free from my past.* The banging seemed to get even louder coming from the front door to the bunker.

I flicked off the light and made my way back to the bed and smothered myself in blankets. I pulled my legs up to my chest and hugged my knees for dear life as my tears fell. *Fred left me. He must have seen there wasn't any hope left. I don't want to die here alone either. I would have left me too. How had I become so estranged from the age of thirteen until now? I used to have so many friends even outside of camp. People actually cared about me. And now look at me. Any second one of the Passions is going to bust that door wide open and then my life will be over. I will be slaughtered as the lonely coward I am. Let them come. I don't care anymore. Fred is gone.* My thoughts fell with my tears as I closed my eyes tight and waited to die.

The banging got louder and louder on the metal door and then stopped. I could hear the metal creaking of the door. Then I could hear heavy footsteps running down the stairs but I didn't look up. I kept my head full of tears down in my hands. *This is it. This is how my life ends. I am ready.*

12

"Hey now, it's okay. We had forgotten someone upstairs and I couldn't let him be dinner." Fred's voice was deep but soft. And I could hear the strong purring in his arms.

The light was on and here was Fred, holding my grumpy old coon-cat that actually looked like he was smiling. That cat was never happy; since the moment he came to live with me from my estranged Great Uncle Charles.

"You went back for Halloween?" I said in a hush as the tears flowed and I pet the black cat who seemed content in Fred's arms.

"Boy was he ever lucky I fished him out from under the bed in time. I had to compel him to come to me." Fred said and then chuckled in a hushed voice.

I wiped my face as the cat jumped down to waiting bowls of food and water. I just looked in amazement at Fred and then hugged him.

"What's all this? Did you think I could ever abandon such a beautiful captor? Nope, I choose Stockholm syndrome. How could I be free, knowing I could have a lovely woman torturing me for the rest of my life?" His thick accent came back as he whispered in my ear and suddenly I wished he was in his favorite kilt.

I looked at him and smiled in complete enchantment.

"Thank you for saving Halloween. He's such a timid cat. I can't believe I forgot about him. He always hides." I whispered and melted in Fred's strong arms.

His neck, his arms, everything about him; felt warm against my skin. I embraced him tighter than hugging a long lost relative. The side of his neck smelt sweeter than summer honey and springtime lilacs. And I didn't stop myself as I kissed his strong muscles, over and over. And then moved to his cheeks and his face; saving his lips for a long kiss.

When Fred kissed me back it felt like the earth moved my soul. If I hadn't been on the bed; I would have collapsed on the floor breathless. I reached to my neck and snapped the key free. I quickly unclasped his silver bracelet and threw it far away from us.

His slashed arm and open burned flesh instantly healed and a fire grew in Fred's eyes.

As the ceiling crashed from above, it sounded like the roof was going to come down on us once again. But Fred didn't stop kissing me and I kissed him right back. My built up needs and desires got the best of me and seemed to melt our clothes off.

With the eerie screaming of the Passions from the ceiling also came our beautiful song of rising vocals in a mending of broken hearts.

I couldn't get enough of Fred. I wanted everything about him. I wanted every last drop of his being; every taste of him. I wanted to devour his soul. He mirrored me and ravished my skin with licks and kisses. Even as Hell seemed to be coming to destroy our world, our bodies moved in only the rhythmic motion of lovers. Faster and faster, pushing and pushing the need for our bodies to become one. Then we both erupted in an explosion of raptured fireworks. And it felt like I had died and went to heaven as Fred collapsed still pulsating inside of me.

All my spirit could feel was his engorged thumping heart that raced with my own needful heart. And the three unspoken words hung in the air between us, which I had just realized with every climax. We rolled in the sheets of ecstasy and made unabashed love as the banging above our heads grew louder and louder.

🌱🌱🌱

I collapsed on his chest and lay in his arms and his fingers traced the length of one of my arms and he kissed my nose. I looked up to his glowing eyes and the warmest smile I had ever seen on anyone. *I really am clueless about how amazing Fred is. And to think he used to scare everyone at Silver Lake Camp.*

"Jenna my Darling, I really have to save us or else the roof will come down on us." His sultry voice still reminded me of a pirate but I could hear the endearment in his growl.

I think I had the foggy brain of a lovesick puppy as I suddenly heard the crashing above. I nodded to him but hugged him tighter.

His eyes went a whole other level of supernatural then held the flame inside as he spoke ten octaves deeper. "Jenna I have to go before we are killed. Get dressed my love and I will be back before you know it."

I nodded again this time as he kissed my hands before removing each one from around his waist. He got up and walked towards the center of the room by the table and then transformed in front of me to a nine foot tall werewolf. He looked very demon-like as his paw-like hands had six inch claws on each finger.

As he placed his giant paw-like foot on the first step; I ran over to him and hugged him from behind. His fur was like cashmere and it had a shiny onyx like quality. As he turned around he picked me up in his arms and I looked at him in awe. Here he was this beautiful magical being that looked vicious but held all the heart and more of any man I had ever known.

He was much more.

"I love you Frederik Dangers. Please come home to me." I said with tears out of my eyes at the thought this might be our last moment together.

My heart sank as he gently set me down and placed a kiss on my cheek. I held his paw-like hand tight and kissed it. Then I moved his hand to my heart as the tears cascaded down. I didn't just want to say the words. I wanted him to feel my love through my heart beating wild for only his.

"It will be okay my love. We have always had a destiny together and no one can take you away from me. Now that I have found the other half of my soul, we will always be together." His voice still ten octaves lower and spooky melted my heart.

His bushy tail gently touched my face to catch a tear and then I watched him ascend the stairwell. I realized I was in love with a legendary beast. He was the stuff that fairy tales, magical fantasies, and campfire stories were made of. And he was made of all the stardust and galaxies in-between. He was everything all at once. And he was mine. He looked back and blew me a kiss; and then disappeared with the creak of the metal door.

I could hear the weird, eerie screaming along with the new growling and howling of wolves. *They had come. His family has come. Fred is an identical twin. I wonder if that means Darion is a werewolf too?*

On that last thought, I quickly got dressed and then put my coat and mittens on. I looked around the room for anything I could use as a weapon as an absolute last resort. *Violence is my last resort.* But it seemed days ago I was thinking that very same thing.

I paused to reflect on if I hadn't gotten to the revolver first. *I would be still on the floor of the apartment if he hadn't missed. That's behind me now. Wish though I hadn't left the gun in the cabin. It could've been useful right now just as much as it was then.*

13

The avalanche of noises cascading above the ceiling sent shivers down my spine as my soulmate was up there and possibly our death loomed overhead. I wondered how long Fred could fight them off. I could hear the wolf calls and knew there were others but the extent of the screaming from the Passions was overbearing to the howling.

Even in this small cavern-hole in the ground, it felt more like a casket than a sanctuary as I listened to the banging on the entrance door. I looked up to the metal being thudded and then around the room. I was going to have to defend myself down here or brave the unknown upstairs. There were no other choices as I heard the howling stop.

Finding a spear in the bunker storage I started on the staircase slowly making my way to the top with my heart dragging behind me. *Fred is brave, I'm not. I don't want to fight anymore. I just want peace but my heart has to find Fred and make sure he's okay. Who knows how many Passions are up there with him. God I hope Fred is successful and if he isn't…Well I can't think like that right now…God I hope he is okay.*

Suddenly the door burst open with a loud metal clang and my weak heart leapt through my chest. My mouth dropped as I seen the branches grab hold of me and drag me through the door. I squinted as the sun was in my eyes and the burning stare of massive red eyes. My throat went dry as the screaming at me began and I see Fred on the ground with some blood coming through his back.

Something in me snapped.

With my free hand holding the spear, I got my upside down bearings and I screamed back in anger at the humanoid-tree that knew no words but only spoke hatred as it dangled me. I kicked and swung off it's branch eyeing the exposed black heart that had shredded splinters around it. The trunk was ravaged with claw marks and held an incomplete task. Fred lay on the ground in a mass of unmoving black fur and splinters of wood surrounding him.

The giant redwood drew back as it expressed shock from my angry screaming. Once it brought me back to devour me as it's black tongue slithered across my head; I sliced it with my spear. And as I was being dropped I plunged my spear into the humanoid-tree's soulless heart that popped with a black explosion of toxic blood that burned the ground that it touched. The Passion whelped as it crunched down, falling on top of the knee deep spear in its chest.

The humanoid-tree's tar-filled sap oozed and I watched as the hatred dimmed out of its eyes and the red disappeared to the depths of the shadows. I stilled for a moment in a pause at what I had just done and then ran over to Fred.

"God Fred. Please, please don't leave me. I need you. My love, please come back to me." I grabbed his body and cradled him in my arms while the Passion started catching fire in a self-igniting blue-purple magical smoke.

I reached and grabbed the spear from it's toppled over body slowly going up in flames. It was as if the trees toed roots were kindling.

Using the flame I heated the spear and flipped over Fred's torn body and seared his wounds shut. With a long howl his eyes popped open as he sputtered and coughed another howl.

"My Hero." He whispered as he looked into my eyes and flashed me that dazzling smile with larger than life canines.

I knew other people would have been frightened. But I wasn't.

I dropped the spear and started kissing and hugging him. I cradled him in my arms.

"I didn't know if it would work. I thought I lost you again. I have lost so many people. I don't think I could bare even the thought of losing you. Don't do that again." I said more serious as I looked into his glowing yellow eyes.

"Yes Ma'am. Besides that really hurts you know when you burn me like that." He growled and winked but I was lost in the moment of almost the pure devastation of losing him.

"I was saving your life, I had to. You were…" I stuttered as my tears flowed down and he placed one large clawed finger on my lips delicately to stop me from talking.

"What I mean is. Thank you for saving my life again." He whispered in his deep growl of a voice that seemed so surreal and spooky and I loved every inch of him.

I kissed him over and over and hugged him as he hugged me tight. Then I paused and looked at him as I sat now on his lap looking into his yellow predator eyes.

"So I guess that means you owe me again eh?" I said and smiled.

"I guess so. Jeeze I don't know how I am ever going to pay off this debt." He growled sheepishly shrugging but winked at me again.

"I know. I was just thinking. I mean I have saved you a lot and who knows; there might be other werewolves who could look after me better?" I said and elbowed him with a smile.

"Hey that hurts. Easy now you'll turn me into a kitten instead of the ferocious monster I am." He said in his deeper octave voice loud enough that nearby birds flew away.

"Frederik Dangers I have no doubt in my mind that you have always been a kitten my love." I said and hugged him warmly.

"Well don't let that get out. I have a reputation for being nasty that I have to uphold." His deep voice sounded frightening and humorous as I smiled and kissed his cheek.

"Yes you do, my big scary monster." I whispered while he held me close to his thudding heart that radiated to mine.

🌿🌿🌿🌿

14

We were creatures of the night finally free from the cabin's restraints. Free to live, free to love, and free to have a real family. Fred welcomed me the Blue Moon Society and everyone was so kind and inviting; it was hard to ever imagine these beautiful people were creatures from campfire legends.

There were tables and tables of people dressed informally but dazzling all the same. Little lights looked like stars strung around each orange table cloth lit with candle center pieces and all kinds of food. My dear old Halloween was being cuddled and adored by the little children that played in and out of the tables.

The food wasn't processed it was all organic and I smelt the aroma of a certain rabbit stew I knew I was going to beg Fred to make me again even though we'd been eating it for the last couple of days on our honeymoon.

"So this is the villain that stole my terrifying brother's heart. You've tamed the great wild beast so I've heard. How was the honeymoon?" Darion chuckled as he hugged me like old friends do when they haven't seen each other for a long time.

His clean shaven face and blond hair dazzled in the sunlight and I seen the resemblance clearly for the first time in my life after Fred cut his hair short and cleaned up for our wedding. They really were identical twins. It's just Fred always had a five-a-clock shadow even when he was fifteen.

"Actually, he's my kitten and I'm his…" I started to say with a smile as Fred placed his finger gently on my mouth and gave me a wink.

"Sorry, you're going to have to put any questions in writing beforehand. Yes, she's my true love and we had a grand time. Short and sweet. Feels good to be back on our land where we don't have to hide or fight to survive." Fred's voice sounded like his grumpy pirate-self as he held a hint of an accent from long ago and it was as smooth as low grade sand paper. *God do I love listening to him speak. I could listen all day long.*

"I know since the Passions have been living a happy existence the rage has been gone from the world. The woods have been so peaceful and back to the loveliness it always has been." Rachel said to me and I was just in awe of her and Darion, happily married with their three kids running around and one more on the way.

"Rachel my dearest friend, it's been so long. I was so happy to find out you were alive and that Darion had married you. This is a perfect wedding gift. My beautiful friend; God have I missed you." I said as I hugged Rachel so tight and let some tears loose from my soft minded heart.

"I'm sorry. We had to fake my death with the grizzly bear attack.

And I was dying until Darion saved me and Tommy." Rachel said as she smiled brightly with the blue sapphire wedding ring on her finger shining through the sunlight and I showed her my giant blood moonstone ring that had never left my hand since the day Fred placed it on my finger.

"Can someone pass the chicken?" Tommy's deep voice was melodic as he had his guitar strung on his shoulder just like from campfire days.

Tommy stole kisses from Lucy and gently kissed her growing baby bump. They looked at each other and whispered sweetly to one another. I loved seeing my friend's happiness match my own.

"It is a pleasure to see Lucy and Tommy together. It is so amazing how the course of our lives have changed us and through hard times made us stronger." I said and I walked with Rachel and Lucy to a bench that overlooked the lake.

The guys caught up with each other and had fun lawn bowling. Lucy and Rachel compared baby bumps while we all drank sweet tea under a willow. And I couldn't be happier for my friends. Both women seemed so much more happier than even our campfire marshmallow filled days. I knew exactly how they felt. It was completeness. Like finally rainbows and sunshine could reign supreme forever more in our lives.

Arabella stopped playing with the other children and came over to bring me flowers. And I kissed her sweet face before she ran off to play again. I felt blessed to have adopted her with Fred, and was happy to have a family of my own.

Suddenly a hush grew across the field and I saw a familiar face through the crowd that made my eyes swell up with love. I got up and walked over to hug my Great Uncle Charles Callaghan who was the other black sheep of our family and whom I had missed dearly.

"Dear Uncle Charles, you are here? It's so good to see you alive. I have missed you." I said as I hugged him tightly.

"Thank you honey. I have missed you too. I am so glad you could be a part of our family. Our Society. I will catch up with you soon Baby Girl, I just have to make a toast. Enjoy your dinner with Fred. He's an amazing fellow and I couldn't be any happier about your marriage." Charles said and his deep voice sounded regal as he strolled up to the small flowery podium.

As my Great Uncle Charles walked everyone bowed their heads as he went by with his best friend Bob Dangers by his side. It seemed to me that I didn't know my Great Uncle at all. Someone told me he was our fearless Alpha and the one who had rescued the others from the Barracks Mills and other corporate plants.

Bob had always seemed scarier than the movies but he dazzled the crowd with magic and pulled some roses out of Fred's baseball hat. We all cheered him on and Fred just winked at his Dad, who winked back.

I looked over at Rachel and Darion's kids playing with Halloween who was being spoiled of ear scratches and pets. My grumpy cat who at one time had hated everyone, absolutely adored the attention. A hush grew over the crowd as Charles raised his glass and taped the microphone to see if it was working.

"Good afternoon everyone. I am so glad you could all make it to this special occasion in celebrating my niece's eloped wedding to Fred Dangers and celebrating our newest members into the Blue Moon Society. All of us sitting at this outdoor picnic couldn't be more perfect than all the stars in the galaxy. What a bunch of harsh years we have all endured, with so many hellish experiences from this changed world. But one thing always endures that no one can take from us, even as centuries will come and go. And that is family, friendship and love surviving death until eternity and back again." Charles cleared his throat as it changed a couple of octaves deeper and his eyes glowed red of a true Alpha.

"Please raise your glasses in a toast to our family. I wish to thank everyone for coming to this reuniting ceremony and soon to be a yearly tradition. Thank you to all our new members who have joined our humble family. May you only find peace under the protected evergreens, rivers and the great Silver Lake of our land. Whether you live with us forever or venture far away to explore; come back every now and again. You will always be welcomed with open arms. You'll always have a home and you'll always have the love of your pack. Cheers Everyone." Charles said with his deep scratchy voice as the Leader of the Pack and turned to smile at his best friend Bob while toasting everyone seated at the thousands of tables.

Everyone raised their glasses of orange juice while I raised my water and said "Cheers" in unison.

Orange juice wasn't agreeing with my stomach lately but I smiled at everyone's glowing faces. I looked at Fred beside me and down at my baby bump that had his hand gently rubbing my growing stomach. Life was simply perfect. We didn't have to hide here and no one was chasing us especially since the Passions were part of the same magic as the werewolves.

I couldn't believe how I had ever lived without Fred by my side. I couldn't have imagined in my wildest dreams how wonderful my life would have turned out. *I wish I had hit Fred with my car a lot sooner.*

As I kissed his cheek my eyes glowed as he kissed me back. *I wish you would have hit me with your car sooner too, my Dove.* His thoughts were sweet and his voice was soft and loving in my head. Everyone turned and smiled at our cherished thoughts and Bob even deeply chuckled out loud.

The sun streamed down on us and butterflies floated freely amongst the tables. The large camp bonfire was now going on in the background while children played and roasted marshmallows. It was the amazing twilight of another great day in the heaven of the Blue Moon Society.

The songbirds and loons started calling out.

The music was lively through the crowd from Tommy playing on his guitar and singing with Darion. People danced to their favorite rock tunes from before the world had changed.

It was simply perfect. The summer sun set with hues of pink, purple and orange; like someone had painted a masterpiece of brush strokes through the clouds. The fireflies glowed among the wild flowers. On the breeze all I could smell was the heavy scent of Fred's musky cologne off his skin and the wild roses he placed beside my bed every night.

♠The End♠

Acknowledgments

I would really like to express my sincere gratitude to; The Universe, my fans, family, and friends. Its fine people like you that give struggling authors a chance; and read their wonderful stories given to the world. Thank you again!

I would also like to thank my mechanics and my friends Eric Heldman and Jay Flowers at Cormier Good Year Obsentia, in Trenton, Ontario. Thank you for always being great friends and taking care of my car. I am so appreciative that you are lights in the world and practice random acts of kindness every day. Thank you again for not suing me for killing off your characters in future novels! Their website is here if you want some kind individuals helping you with your auto needs and are in the Quinte West Area: https://www.trentontire.ca/

Thank you for reading! I really hope you have liked my book. Thank you again! Please add a short review and let me know what you thought! If you would like to join my author page please join here on FB: https://www.facebook.com/profile.php?id=10008921381 0837

Or you can email me directly to chat at: a.l.secordauthor@gmail.com *. You can also request to be added to my mailing list for future updates of novels and freebies. Your information will never be shared; it will only be added to future emails from me, on updates about my books coming out and tips on writing Dark Fantasy Romance.*

Thanks again and Let your light shine bright!

ABOUT THE AUTHOR

A.L. Secord is a pen name for the author APRIL SECORD. She enjoys many genres but Dark Fantasy Romance is her *Passion*. She is just one being of light, trying to let other beings of light shine their light too. She enjoys motivating people to fulfill their dreams and to dream big! She loves learning new things, and occasionally burning food for the ones she loves. She is an author; a proud mother and an avid adventurer of the unknown; on her many pursuits for greater happiness and Bigfoot.

OF
THE
STARS
A.L. SECORD

A DARK FANTASY
BEFORE THE
FEAR OF
THE MOON
A.L. SECORD
WEREWOLF CAMPFIRE SERIES BOOK ONE

NOTES ON GRIEF: SELF CARE WITH FLAIR
CHOOSE
HAPPINESS
APRIL SECORD

A DARK FANTASY ROMANCE
BEFORE THE
HEART OF
THE MOON
A.L. SECORD
WEREWOLF CAMPFIRE SERIES BOOK TWO

A DARK FANTASY ROMANCE
BEFORE THE
CHAOS OF
THE MOON
A.L. SECORD
WEREWOLF CAMPFIRE SERIES BOOK THREE